Wanda's Freckles

BARBARA AZORE • Illustrated by GEORGIA GRAHAM

Tundra Books

Wanda had freckles. Lots of freckles. Freckles on her legs. Freckles on her arms. Freckles sprinkled across her cheeks and nose like raindrops on a windowpane.

Her three-year-old cousin Myles, who sometimes muddled his words, called them sparkles.

Her mother said the sun brought them because Wanda had very fair skin.

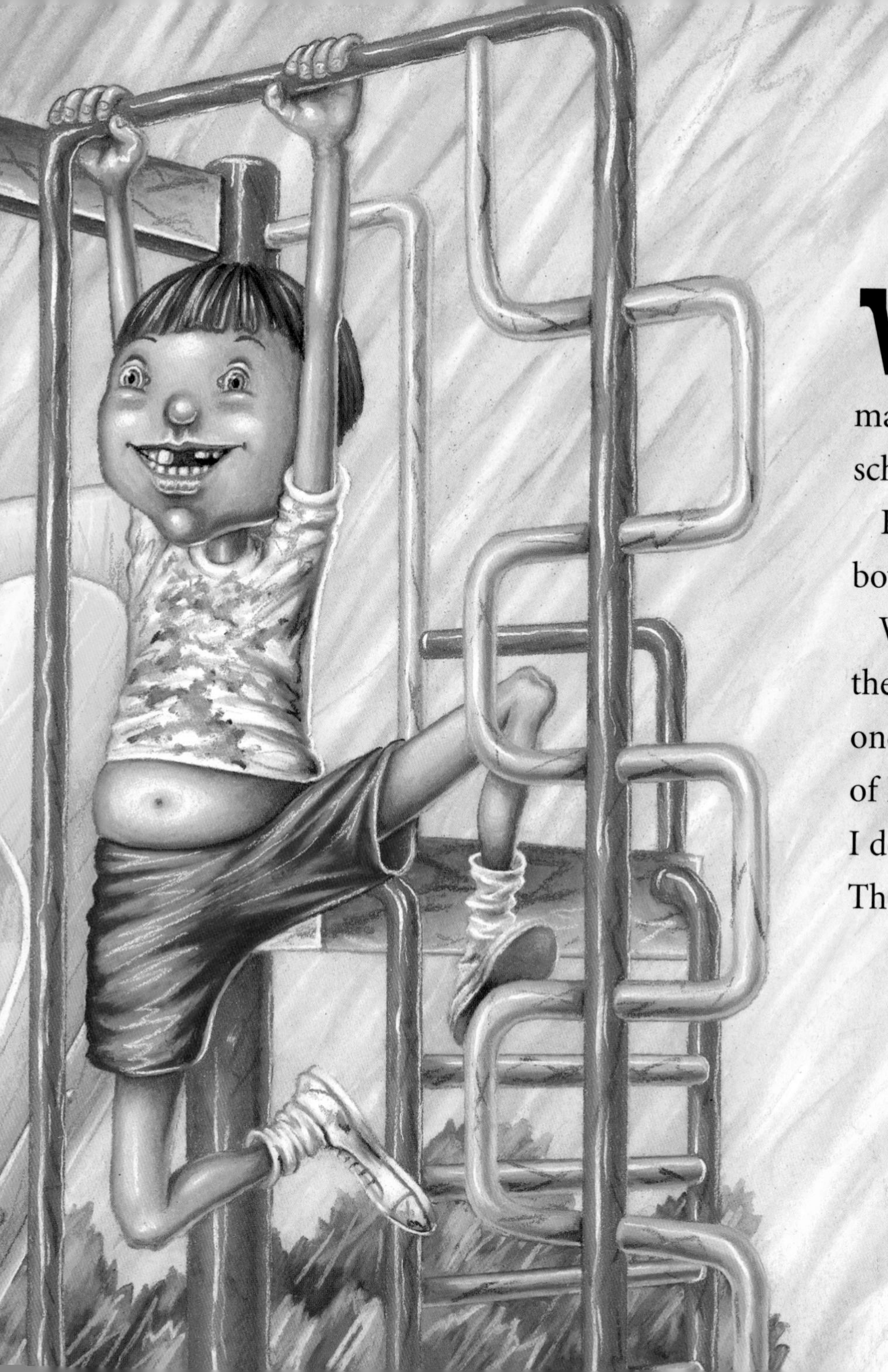

Wanda liked her freckles. They made her feel special. No one else in school had as many freckles as she did.

But, one day in the park, a group of boys pointed and laughed at her.

Wanda walked over to find out what they were laughing at. As she got near, one of the boys, his arm out in front of him, called, "Don't come near me. I don't want to catch your spots!" The other boys giggled.

Wanda stopped, puzzled. She glared at the boy and said, "I don't have spots!"

"What are those things on your face then?" the boy asked.

Wanda put her hands to her cheeks and blushed. "Those aren't spots," she declared. "They're freckles. *You* can't have freckles. Only people with fair skin have freckles."

The boys fell about laughing again.

"Freckles, smeckles," said another boy. "I'm glad I can't have them. I don't want to be spotty."

He turned around, and all the boys ran away chanting, "Spotty, spotty, we don't want to be spotty."

Wanda was upset. She ran home and told her mother what the boys had said.

"Don't take any notice of them, dear. They're just being silly," Mother replied.

But Wanda couldn't forget. She didn't like being laughed at.

Slowly she climbed the stairs on the way to her room. When she passed her parents' bedroom, the door was open. Wanda saw Mother's lipsticks on the dressing table.

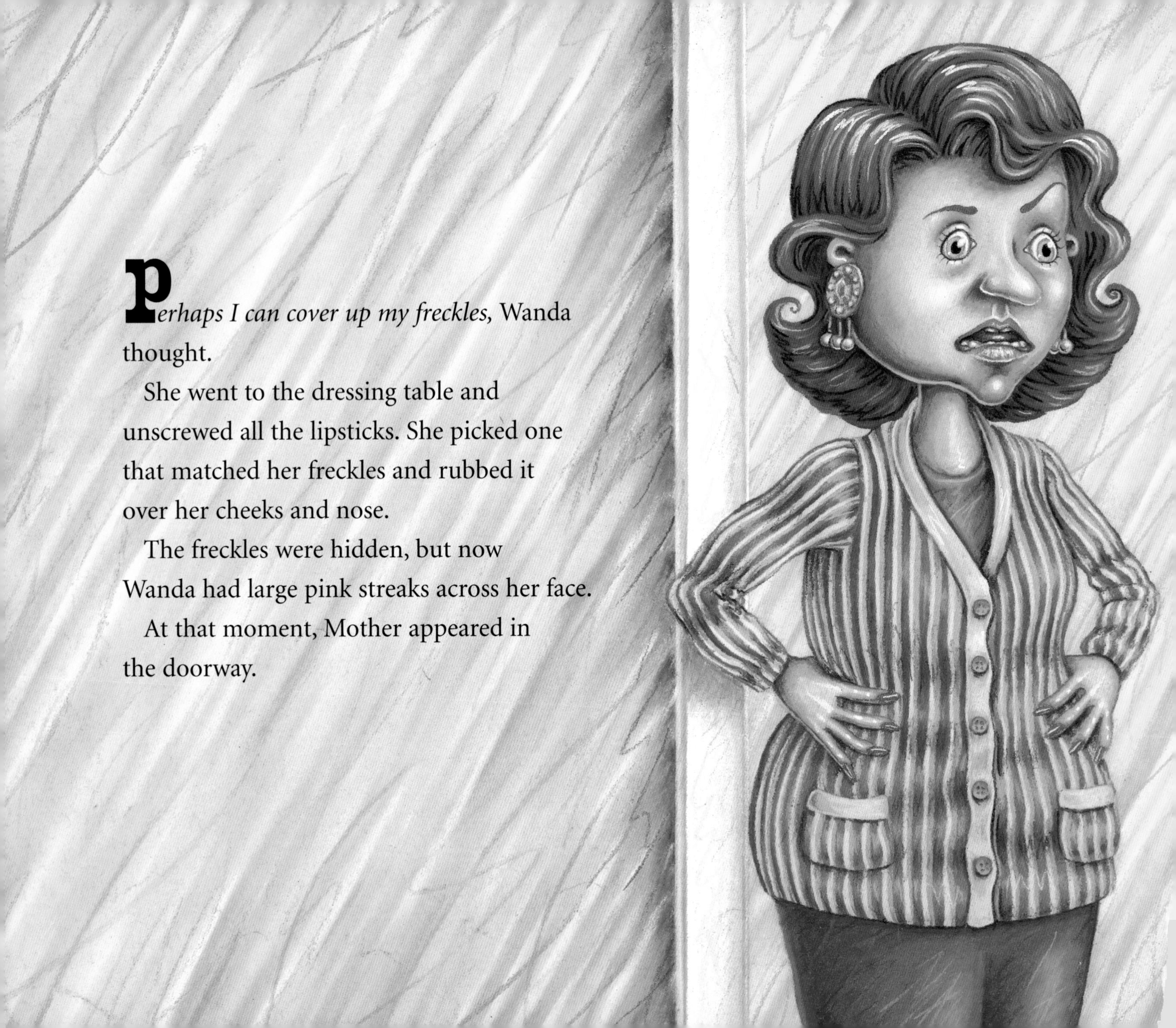

P*erhaps I can cover up my freckles,* Wanda thought.

She went to the dressing table and unscrewed all the lipsticks. She picked one that matched her freckles and rubbed it over her cheeks and nose.

The freckles were hidden, but now Wanda had large pink streaks across her face.

At that moment, Mother appeared in the doorway.

"What are you doing?" Mother asked, marching toward Wanda.

"I'm trying to hide my freckles."

Mother opened a jar of cream and rubbed it over Wanda's face. Then she gently wiped it off with a tissue.

The lipstick disappeared and Wanda's freckles reappeared.

"There," said Mother. "That's the face I love. Now leave my makeup alone, young lady."

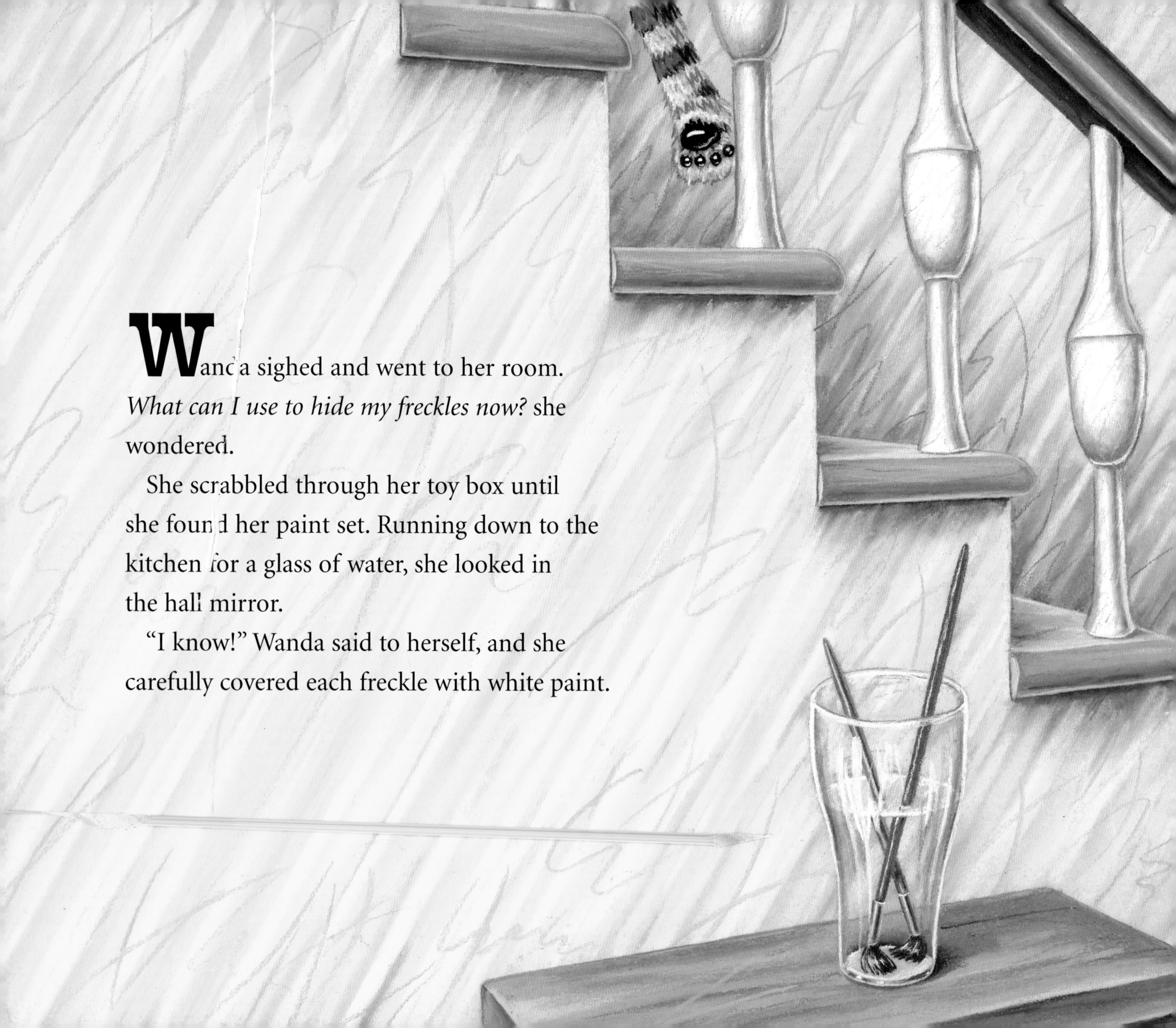

Wanda sighed and went to her room. *What can I use to hide my freckles now?* she wondered.

She scrabbled through her toy box until she found her paint set. Running down to the kitchen for a glass of water, she looked in the hall mirror.

"I know!" Wanda said to herself, and she carefully covered each freckle with white paint.

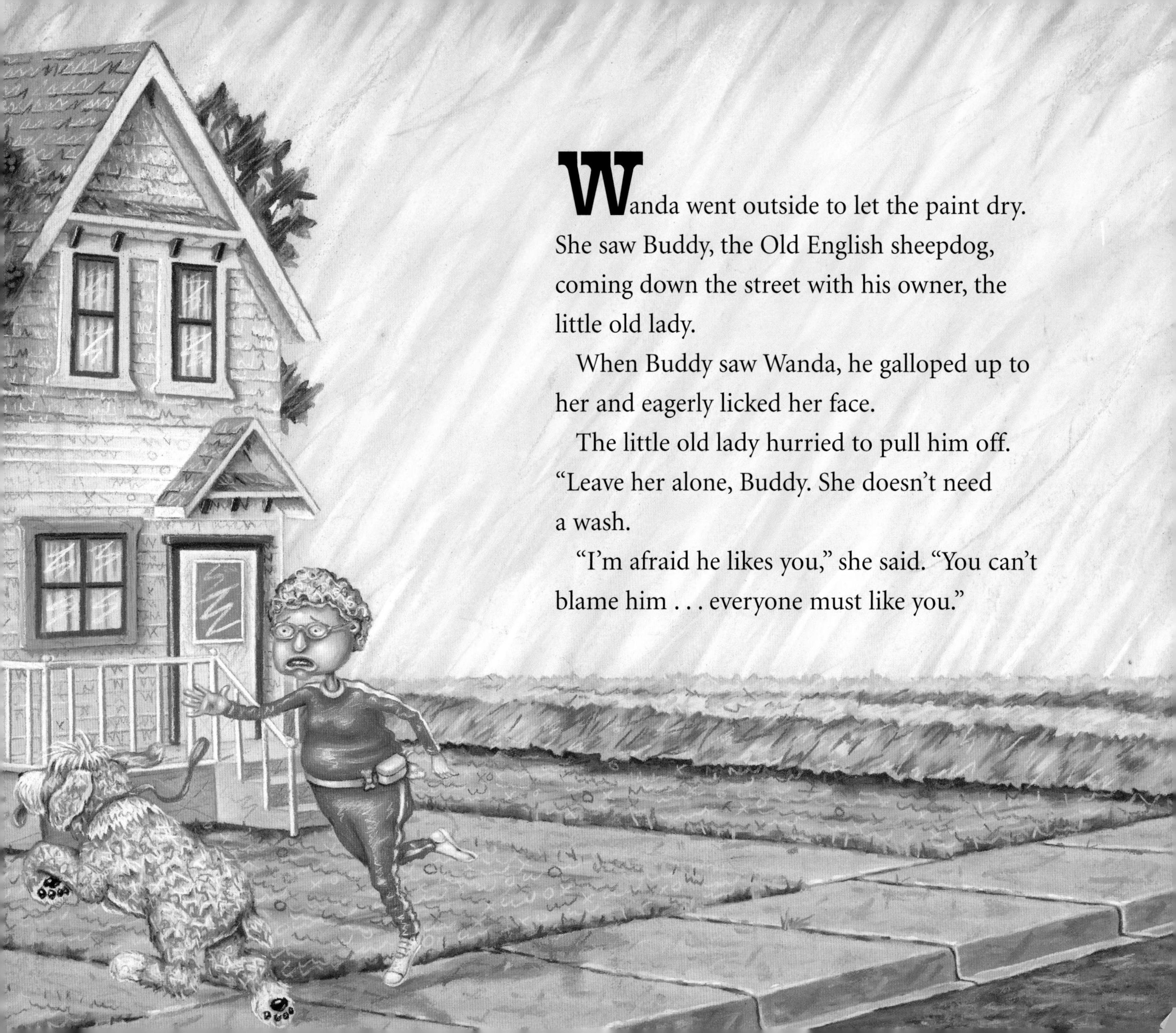

Wanda went outside to let the paint dry. She saw Buddy, the Old English sheepdog, coming down the street with his owner, the little old lady.

When Buddy saw Wanda, he galloped up to her and eagerly licked her face.

The little old lady hurried to pull him off. "Leave her alone, Buddy. She doesn't need a wash.

"I'm afraid he likes you," she said. "You can't blame him . . . everyone must like you."

Wanda went into the house to wipe her face. Looking in the mirror, she saw that Buddy had licked off all the paint. Her freckles were back!

Sadly, she couldn't think of any other way to get rid of them.

At bedtime, Wanda went into the bathroom to brush her teeth. When she picked up the toothpaste, she saw a word she recognised: "WHITE." She spelled out the other letters: "WHITE-EN-ING."

Perhaps the toothpaste will whiten my freckles! she thought. Wanda squeezed out a blob and scrubbed it into her cheeks. When she rinsed it off, her cheeks had turned pink and her freckles were brighter than ever.

Wanda was disappointed, but then she remembered what the little old lady had said. She had lots of friends, and those boys *were* just being silly. If she didn't have freckles, she would not be herself. She liked herself just the way she was.

Wanda brushed her teeth and climbed into bed. In a few minutes, she was fast asleep, dreaming of boys covered in big red spots.

For every child who is different

B.A.

For the boys in my grade-four class who made fun of me:

You were great inspiration for this book.

G.G.

Published in Canada by Tundra Books,
75 Sherbourne Street, Toronto, Ontario M5A 2P9

Published in the United States by Tundra Books of Northern New York,
P.O. Box 1030, Plattsburgh, New York 12901

Library of Congress Control Number: 2008910103

Library and Archives Canada Cataloguing in Publication

Azore, Barbara
Wanda's freckles / Barbara Azore ; illustrated by Georgia Graham.

ISBN 978-0-88776-862-0

I. Graham, Georgia, 1959- II. Title.

PS8601.Z67W368 2009 jC813'.6 C2008-907126-3

We acknowledge the financial support of the Government of Canada through the Book Publishing Industry Development Program (BPIDP) and that of the Government of Ontario through the Ontario Media Development Corporation's Ontario Book Initiative.

We further acknowledge the support of the Canada Council for the Arts and the Ontario Arts Council for our publishing program.

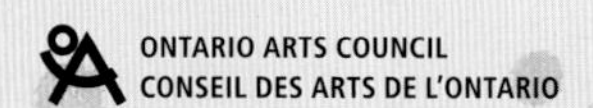

Medium: chalk pastel on paper

Design: Terri Nimmo

Printed in China

1 2 3 4 5 6 14 13 12 11 10 09